THE
CARROT SEED

THE
CARROT SEED

Story by Ruth Krauss

Pictures by Crockett Johnson

HarperCollins*Publishers*

Copyright 1945 by Harper & Row, Publishers, Inc.
Text copyright renewed 1973 by Ruth Krauss
Illustrations copyright renewed 1973 by Crockett Johnson
Manufactured in China. All rights reserved.
For information address HarperCollins Children's Books,
a division of HarperCollins Publishers,
195 Broadway, New York, NY 10007.
ISBN 0-06-023350-8. — ISBN 0-06-023351-6 (lib. bdg.)
ISBN 0-06-443210-6 (pbk.) LC Number 45-4530
19 20 21 SCP 40 39 38 37 36

A little boy planted
a carrot seed.

His mother said, "I'm afraid
it won't come up."

His father said, "I'm afraid it won't come up."

And his big brother said,

"It won't come up."

Every day the little boy pulled up the weeds around the seed and sprinkled the ground with water.

But nothing came up.

And nothing came up.

Everyone kept saying it wouldn't come up.

But he still pulled up the weeds around it every day and sprinkled the ground with water.

And then, one day,

a carrot came up

just as the little boy

had known it would.